Don't Get Me In Trouble!

by Steven Kroll

with pictures by Marvin Glass

Crown Publishers, Inc.

To Sydney Butchkes and Betty Prashker
who made it possible.

Published by Crown Publishers, Inc.,
225 Park Avenue South, New York, New York 10003, and
represented in Canada by the Canadian MANDA Group
CROWN is a trademark of Crown Publishers, Inc.
Manufactured in Japan
Library of Congress Cataloging-in-Publication Data
Kroll, Steven.
   Don't get me in trouble.
   Summary: Whenever Mickey thinks up fun things to do, it is his friend Jake who
gets into trouble, until Mickey finds out that this situation might change.
[1. Behavior—Fiction.   2. Friendship—Fiction] I. Glass, Marvin, ill.   II. Title
PZ7.K9225Do 1987   [E]   87-13391   ISBN 0-517-56724-5
10 9 8 7 6 5 4 3 2 1
First Edition

Mickey and Jake were friends.
In school and out, they stuck together.

The problem was Mickey loved thinking up crazy things to do on the weekends. And Jake always ended up in trouble.

The day they were dangling by one paw from Mickey's tree house, Jake lost his grip and tumbled into Dolly Dalmatian's flower bed.

They got out of there fast.

"Hey, Mickey," said Jake, "next time, please don't get me in trouble!"

Mickey grinned. "Don't worry, Jake. Trust me."

The next weekend, Mickey thought it would be a great idea if they snitched a few dog bones from Connie Collie's Café.

Mickey grabbed a bone. He was
halfway down the block when he noticed
Jake wasn't with him. He ran back to
find Connie Collie's cousin clobbering Jake
with a rolling pin.

He grabbed Jake's paw, and the two pups
ran off down the street.

Panting to keep up, Jake said, "Please, Mickey,
next time, don't get me in trouble."

Mickey shrugged. "No problem, Jake, no problem."

The next weekend they didn't get to do anything. Jake was grounded for snitching dog bones from Connie Collie's Café.

The weekend after that, Mickey suggested they go swimming at the old swimming hole.

"What a good idea," said Jake, tripping over a root. "Nothing can get me in trouble swimming."

When they arrived at the old swimming
hole, lots of dogs were paddling around.

"I'm going to dive off that rock,"
said Mickey.

"Me, too," said Jake.

Together they climbed the rock. "I'll go
first," said Mickey. "Watch this."

He did a graceful, swooping swan dive.
Everyone applauded as he rose to the
surface and waved.

Suddenly Jake got very scared. He
clutched his knees, closed his eyes,
and jumped.

KABOOM! He landed in the water, right
on top of Tina Terrier.

"Help!" sputtered Tina.

Rupert Retriever, the lifeguard, rushed to
the rescue. He grabbed hold of Tina and
carried her to shore.

Then he turned to Jake. "OUT!" he said.

Jake hung his head. But Mickey was
right beside him. "Come on," he said.
"Let's go to Puppy Playland."

Jake stopped in his tracks. "You're not
going to get me in trouble again?"
"Don't be silly. It'll be fun."

All the way to Puppy Playland, Mickey couldn't stop telling Jake about how wonderful it was going to be. When they got there, Jake saw he was right. Rides zoomed up and down and around. Dogs were everywhere, playing ringtoss and darts and eating ice cream and cotton candy.

Mickey and Jake bought their tickets from the barker. Then they bought some ice cream and cotton candy.

"Are you sure I'm not going to get in trouble?" Jake asked.

"Of course not," said Mickey. "Let's go to the fun house!"

In the fun house, Jake looked in the mirrors and was fat and then skinny and then all squooshed together in the middle. He stumbled through the rolling barrel, and the magic carpet slide slid him across the floor.

But Mickey was right. He didn't get in any trouble.

When Jake got outside, he smiled.
  "You see," said Mickey. "No problem."
  Just then a truck came by, carrying
empty flowerpots. "Let's hitch a ride to the
bumper cars," Mickey said.
  But suddenly the truck hit a bump.

A pot fell off the pile! It landed upside down on Mickey's head!

Mickey didn't know what hit him. He started running in circles.

"Mickey!" said Jake. "Wait! It's just—"

But Mickey wouldn't wait, and Mickey wouldn't listen.

Dogs barked—and scattered left and right. Mickey ran right onto the roller coaster as it was starting off!

"Hang on, Mickey!" Jake yelled.

But Mickey couldn't hear Jake, and he didn't hang on. The roller coaster dove over the top of the hill and thundered down. Mickey flipped, head over heels, into the air. The flowerpot flew off his head…

and he crashed through the roof
of a hot-dog stand. Hot dogs flew
everywhere.

"Crazy mutts, get out of here!"
shouted the vendor.

Jake grabbed Mickey, and they took off.

"I think you got in trouble," Jake said.
"Yeah," said Mickey, "but next weekend—"

Jake smiled. "How about checkers at my house?"
"A *terrific* idea!"
And the next weekend, that's exactly what they did.

juv.   91-888

Kroll, Steven

Don't Get Me In Trouble!

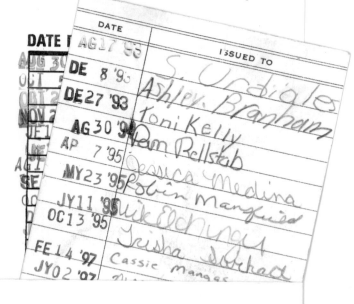

DATE	ISSUED TO
AG17 '93	S. Urdiales
DE 8 '93	Ashley Branham
DE27 '93	Toni Kelly
AG30 '9	Pam Rellstab
AP 7 '95	Jessica Medina
MY23 '95	Robin Manfield
JY11 '95	Nik Elchinal
OC13 '95	Trisha Hitchard
FE14 '97	Cassie Manges
JY02 '97	